The Young GRIZZLY

by PAIGE DIXON

illustrated by
GRAMBS MILLER

Cover by
Richard Amundsun

SCHOLASTIC BOOK SERVICES
NEW YORK • TORONTO • LONDON • AUCKLAND • SYDNEY • TOKYO

12 11 10 9 8 7 6 5 4 3 2 1 1 8 9/7 0 1 2 3/8
01

Printed in the U. S. A.

To Jones
with love

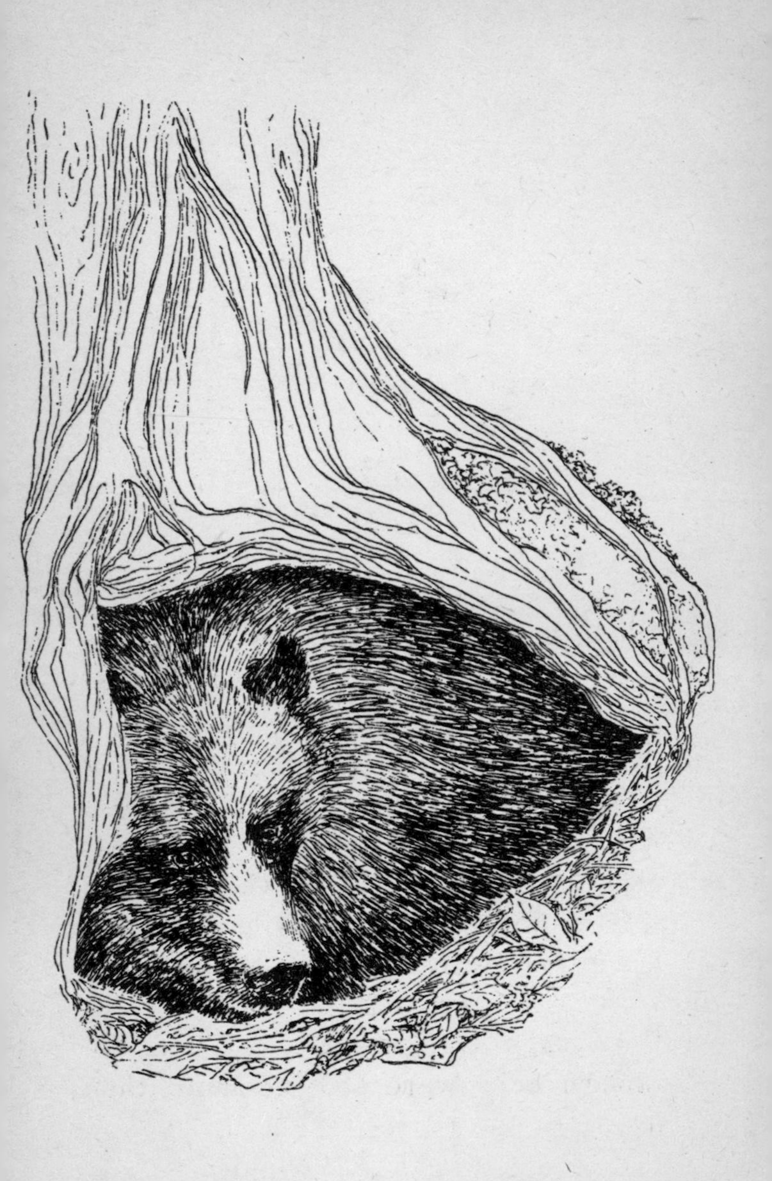

Part I

1

Deep in December the wheat-colored Grizzly stirred in her den. Outside on the eastern slope of the high ridge, snow piled up. She pawed listlessly at the mound of leaves and twigs she had packed into the den in October. It was a big den, close to the timber line. The entrance sloped down, following an underground ledge. The hollow where the bear lay was almost nine feet deep.

Although she had mated in June, the unborn cubs were still no more than three-quarters of an inch long. They would not be born until late January or early February, and when they were born, they would be the size of a chipmunk, blind, toothless, and hairless.

But the big bear was not concerned with unborn cubs now. She pushed away the snow that made a door to her cave and stepped out into the air. Unlike her neighbors the ground squirrels, who fell into a winter sleep so deep their hearts almost stopped beating and their temperature fell almost to the point of death, the bear, like bears everywhere, was a relatively light sleeper, who had awakened several times during the long winter.

Standing outside her den, she wagged her head slowly back and forth to catch whatever smells there were. Her small, dark eyes could not see well, but her sensitive nose and her keen ears told her what she needed to know. There was no scent of man in the air, and that was the only creature she feared.

It was an unseasonably warm day, with a light wind blowing from the west. To provide her with enough fat to see her through the winter, she had eaten almost steadily from May to November, so she was not hungry, but she considered taking a short walk before she went back to the den.

A low roar changed her mind. Clumsily she backed into her cave as an avalanche of snow and rocks shot down over the side of the mountain with a deep sound like sustained thunder. Ice and rocks bounced off the ledge that protected the bear.

Inside the cave, she circled sleepily and lay down again. In a few minutes she was asleep.

2

During the last week in May the big sow bear got to her feet, stepping over the two cubs curled up close to her. The cubs, born in the second day of February, had grown. The female now weighed about 20 pounds, and the male was 5 or 6 pounds heavier. Their dark, rounded eyes were open, and they had cut their first teeth. The male was the color of charcoal, with a silver mantle over his shoulders, and white claws. His sister was the color of cinnamon.

Now as their mother thrust her head

out of the den, sniffing all the scents coming in on the spring breeze, the cubs squealed and tried to hang onto her, worried about what she was up to. They were dragged along when she stepped outside.

The female cub bawled and tried to bury her head in her mother's thick fur. She was alarmed by the outside world. The male was frightened too, but he was also very curious. He let go of his mother and looked down the side of the mountain. Although there were patches of bare ground, the mountain at the height of the den was still mostly covered with snow. Like his mother, he wagged his head slowly back and forth, smelling all the surprising smells. It was almost overwhelming, and for a moment he scampered back to the cave as if he intended to hide inside again. But then he whirled around once more, falling heels over head in his eagerness. His mother was already moving down the side of the mountain, with her long, rolling gait. He had to hurry to keep up with her.

She knew where she was going. In a few minutes she was feeding on glacier lilies, pulling up roots and all. The little silvertip cub tried to imitate his mother, but he didn't like the lilies. It would be another couple of months before the cubs would learn to prefer solid food to their mother's milk.

He cuffed his sister and she went sprawling on a patch of ice, sliding down an incline on her back, squealing at the top of her lungs. He ran after her, and she grabbed his neck with her front paws. They wrestled furiously, almost beside themselves with the excitement of being out in the world. Their mother went on eating, but she kept a close watch. When they moved too far away from her, she woofed and scolded till they came back. The female was not as adventurous as the little male. And twice, when the male didn't mind his mother's command to come back, the big bear went after him and put her big paw on him just hard enough so he would remember. He squealed in protest, but he learned to obey her.

Later in the day she led them down the side of the mountain into a stand of alpine fir. With her tremendous teeth she tore the bark off a tree and licked the sap.

Then she moved on to the next tree, until a whole line of firs had been marked by her teeth.

In another place, further down the mountain, she found big boulders. The little cubs watched her as she turned them over and scooped up ladybugs by the gallon, and, in another place, ants.

The male cub raced up the trunk of a white pine and swayed dangerously on a branch. His sister came partway up, but she was not as reckless as he was.

Peering down from his swinging branch, the cub saw his mother lift her head suddenly and then rear up on her hind legs, to see better. She swung her great head slowly back and forth, searching out the smell she was looking for. Then abruptly she dropped down on all fours and growled a quick command to her cubs. The male didn't want to come down out of the tree, but she barked at him again, and he came. Making sure they stayed close at her heels, she loped up the slope into some heavy brush. The thicket scratched the cubs, but she gathered them in close to her and then turned to face the trail they had just left.

A male Grizzly came slowly up the trail, sniffing the wind. The cubs could hear his long curved claws scratching on rock as he climbed. The wind was blowing toward the mother bear and the cubs. The little male sniffed the strong scent of the old bear on the trail, but the bear failed to discover them. The cub felt fear for the first time in his life, although he wasn't sure what he was afraid of.

Again his curiosity was stronger than his fright. He poked his head through the leaves to watch the big bear climb. He felt his mother's quick spank, but he lingered a moment longer. The big bear stopped on the trail and woofed. After a minute he suddenly leaped into a thick patch of brush and gnarled trees on the other side of the trail and thrashed around furiously, making a great racket. Satisfied finally that there was nothing there, he came out and went on up the trail at a leisurely lope. But before he had gone on, the little cub had noticed the big white patches on the bear's dark-brown chest, and the bear's tremendous size.

3

The cubs were getting bigger. Their mother still never let them out of her sight, but they had learned to eat as she ate, and to be a little more independent. The three of them ranged over an area of 10 or 12 miles, eating all the time. They munched grass and ate glacier lilies and dug up roots. One day when they came to a wide place where an avalanche had ended, they found some small dead animals to add to their vegetable diet, animals killed some time before by a sweeping, roaring destruction of sliding snow. This was the way they liked meat, decomposed and smelling strong.

On another day their mother dug furiously for almost an hour to uncover a ground squirrel. The dirt flew under her heavy paws as she dug into the hard ground. But in the end, the squirrel escaped, and she gave up her digging as suddenly as she had begun it. As the cubs were beginning to discover, half of the fun was in the digging.

Eventually they went far down the mountain, but they stayed away from open areas. The edge of a wooded place, or an already worn trail through woods, attracted them.

One twilight, their mother discovered a hive of bees. She thrust her nose into it, looking for the honey. The angry bees swarmed around her head, but her thick hide protected her. When the cubs tried to get their share, the bees stung them. More thin-skinned than their mother, they squealed with pain and slapped at their faces, running wildly in circles and bumping into each other. Their mother went on eating honey, paying no attention. The cubs rubbed their noses along the ground to ease the pain. Later, when their mother had had enough, they licked honey off her face and paws. But it would be a long time before they would venture to attack a beehive again.

They were learning other things as well. An adult Grizzly bear has almost no enemies, because no other animal is willing to risk those huge slashing claws and that enormous size, but there are certain circumstances that a smart bear learns to avoid. The male cub found that out when he poked an inquisitive nose into a badger's hole and felt an excruciating pain as the badger, who was at home, fastened his teeth on the cub's nose. Bawling with pain, the cub tried to shake the animal loose, but those wickedly sharp teeth hung on.

The mother bear, who was eating buds off some nearby trees, came in a lumbering run to find out what had happened to her cub. A wide swipe of her big paw knocked the badger loose, and another blow killed him. But the cub moaned and squealed for a long time from the pain in his nose.

As the cubs grew bigger, they became more independent, but still they never strayed too far from their mother, for they had learned that she would protect them.

One very hot day in late June, when the black flies and the mosquitoes were as thick as clouds, the mother bear led the cubs down into a hollow where a spring kept the long grass green and wet. She lay down and rolled on her back in the cool wet grass. At first the cubs decided to scamper up a tree, but then the male cub ventured too far out on a limb and fell off. He howled with fright, but after a moment he discovered that the long grass his mother was rolling in felt good. He too went over on his back, his four legs sticking straight up. Gently he moved back and forth, getting his shoulders soaked in the dampness. His sister watched from her place in the tree, her small bright eyes curious. Then she too scampered down and wallowed in the grass.

The male cub was having such a good time, he forgot about how hot it was and how bad the insects had been. He rolled right to the edge of the sleeping spring, getting his coat muddy.

Suddenly his mother got to her feet, faster than he had ever seen her move before. She wagged her head back and forth, sniffing the breeze. Then she stood on her hind legs, trying to see up the slope. The little bear lay on his back, his head cocked to one side to watch her.

Then he too smelled a strange, strong smell that he had never noticed before. His mother gave a quiet but urgent woof and he scrambled to his feet, slipping in the oozing grass. His sister, unaware, still rolled luxuriously, even digging her nose into the wetness. Her mother woofed again, but the little bear didn't hear or didn't take notice. The male stood watching his mother. Her behavior made him afraid, although he didn't know what he was afraid of.

With a quick slap of her paw, the mother cuffed the little female, and then started up the slope, on the opposite side from the trail they had come down. The male loped along at her heels, and finally, still lagging behind, the female came too.

The little bears had to hurry to keep up with the fast pace of their mother. Near the top of the slope, she turned to the left, crossed a broad slab of rock, and went into a thick stand of brush. She hustled the cubs in behind her and then stood facing the trail.

Once again the mother rose up to her full height and moved her head slowly back and forth. Then she dropped to all fours again and checked once more on the cubs. She stood very still, as below them, in the wallow they had just left, there were voices. Shivering at the strange sound and the strong, unfamiliar smell, the little male huddled closer to his mother. The tip of her nose lifted a little, and her lower lip dropped. A wrinkle spread across the bridge of her nose. Leaning against her, he could feel the vibration of what was almost a growl, but there was no sound from her.

"They've been here just recent," a voice said. It was a low voice, but it carried on the still air. "Looks like a sow and two cubs. See them prints?"

Another voice said, "How do you know two?"

"Use your eyes," the man said impatiently. "Look here, and here. They climbed a tree, and one of 'em fell off. See the bent branch, and the bent grass where he landed?"

"We'd better get out of here, Pop. I don't want to run into no Grizzly with cubs. Besides, it's out of season."

"As far as I'm concerned, there's no season on Grizzlies."

"If you got caught..."

"Never been caught yet."

"But you could get caught. Everybody knows..."

The man interrupted. "Don't tell me what everybody knows. You don't know nothing. You don't even know when there's been three bears right before your eyes, can't even read tracks."

"I never said I was a big hunter." The younger voice was angry now. "I don't care about hunting."

"Bears are meant to be hunted. They're vicious animals."

"Cubs too?"

"Cubs too. Cubs grow up to be full-grown bears. You coming with me now, or you going back to camp?"

After a moment of silence, the younger voice said, "I come this far, I might as well stay. But I don't like it."

"You ain't obliged to like it."

The voices stopped. The male cub pressed closer to his mother, and even his sister was quiet. In a moment the man scent grew still stronger, and the little cub wrinkled his nose. He could hear them now, coming up the trail toward the place where they were. He felt the muscles tense in his mother's side. Again she curled her lip back over her great teeth.

When the man spoke again, his voice was so near, it terrified the little bear. "Can't tell if they went straight on up, or what. All this rock don't show anything."

"Listen, Pop, why don't we go back to camp? It's getting late. I don't like this. Those bears could jump us from any of these thickets, and we'd never know what hit us."

"You can go back. I already told you so."

"You come too."

"I'm on the trail of three bears. I ain't about to quit now." His voice grew fainter and a small shower of pebbles slid back down the trail as the two climbed up.

The bears stood perfectly still for a long time. Then the mother bear stepped out onto the trail and started climbing, following the path the two hunters had taken.

The cubs stayed close at their mother's heels as she lumbered up the trail after the two men. In a few minutes they were so close, they could hear an occasional twig snap under the men's boots, and now and then the men's voices, although most of the time they were silent.

Once the male cub caught a glimpse of a jacket as the men rounded a curve in the trail and then dipped down toward a switchback. The big bear stopped until they were out of sight again, then plodded on. The young bear was intensely curious about these strange and alarming creatures. He would have liked to get even closer, to get a better look at them.

His mother stopped abruptly, and both cubs bumped into her. She stepped into a thick clump of brush and twisted Engelmann spruce, and the cubs hustled in after her. The sun was far down in the western sky, and it was close to twilight, the time the bears liked best. In the fading light they were not visible to a casual glance from the trail.

In a minute the two men came back down the trail, no longer keeping their voices low.

"If it wasn't getting dark, I could have caught up with them," the older man said. He paused for a moment, almost alongside the place where the bear stood. "Treacherous critters. Soon as it gets dark, they'll jump you."

"I never heard of that, Pop," the younger one said. "I thought they'd jump you any time they felt scared of you."

The older man turned toward him. "What do you know? You don't know nothing."

"But you can't kill all the bears in the world."

"I can kill as many as I can find."

"A Grizzly ain't easy to kill. Some day one of them will get you."

"I'm smarter than any bear. A man is smarter than a bear, any day in the week." He started down the trail again.

The younger man stood for a moment, looking out across the mountains. Then he sighed. "I don't know, Pop." He said it so softly, his father didn't hear him. Then he followed him down the trail.

4

It was a hot summer day, and the bears had covered a lot of ground in search of food. They had climbed the rocky ridges and roamed the high rolling uplands, stopping whenever they found anything to eat — plants, bark, grass, leaves, and sometimes when they were lucky, a swarm of ants, a rabbit. The two cubs, who now weighed around 70 pounds, the male a little bigger than his sister, had learned to strip the bark from a tree, to hunt for snakes, to dig out a ground squirrel, and to jump for grasshoppers. Life was a constant search for food.

Their mother led them down a steep trail that the male cub could not remember having been on before. A roaring sound grew louder as they came down the side of the hill. A stream that ran close beside them gained force, the water foaming over the rocks, spray flying. The two cubs stopped to thrust their heads into the cold water, but when their mother disappeared, they scampered after her, slipping and sliding on loose gravel. Near the bottom of the steep incline there was a shelf of rock, and here the thunder was very loud as the stream that flung itself down the hill poured over the ledge in a waterfall.

The cubs stopped, surprised. They could not see their mother anywhere. The waterfall thundered, and the air was full of cool mist, some of it in rainbow colors as the sunlight caught the flung spray. It felt deliciously cool after the long walk in the hot sun. The male cub edged closer to the waterfall, then tumbled backward, alarmed by all that noise. He looked around for his mother, and at last he saw the top of her head. Far below them, she was standing at the foot of the waterfall, letting the full force of the water splash on her. The cub squealed with delight, and ran so far down the last part of the hill that he stumbled and pitched head over heels to the bottom. Growling a little, he picked himself up and shook himself. His sister, sliding in a sitting-down position, all four feet held up, crashed into him with a thud and knocked him down again.

Both of them raced over to their mother, and after a few moments of hesitation, they stepped in beside her, skidding on the wet rocks. The impact of the water was startling and at first frightening, but as the cubs learned to brace their feet and keep their balance, they began to enjoy the cool torrent. They stood in the falls for a long time, turning a little now and then to catch the water on their shoulders or on their backs or their chests. The male turned his face up to the water, shutting his eyes tight, but the water streamed into his nose and mouth and made him choke.

When they left the falls, they felt good, their coats cool and wet. They followed the river downstream, and in one place the male cub stepped into the shallows and balanced on a floating log. For a moment he kept his balance, but then the current caught the log and spun it around, and the cub fell over backward into the stream. He shook himself and ran after his mother.

She had stopped at a tall, dead pine, and stretching up to her full height, she reached up and clawed the bark, bit it and scratched it, and rubbed her body against the tree.

When she swung down on all fours again, the two cubs imitated her, reaching up as high as they could on the tree. The male rubbed his chest against the bark and then turned around and rubbed his back wherever it itched.

Now they were very hungry. They followed their mother, loping around the edge of a meadow, heading down the mountainside until they reached a wide stretch of open land. In the distance a herd of cattle grazed. The mother bear stopped and stood up, trying to make out what the animals were. She could see them only as dim shapes, like shadows, across the field. She moved around the field until she was upwind. Then she smelled the cattle and knew what they were. She turned away and led the cubs along the edge of trees, down the slope of the meadow, away from the cattle.

Most of the time the bears followed their own trails, but today the mother ambled along in the shade of the woods that bordered the field, looking for food. In one place she stopped and turned into the woods. She began to dig furiously, overturning great mounds of dirt and hurling rocks away from her. The cubs joined her, doing as she did, without knowing what they were after.

In a few minutes, off to one side, a woodchuck shot out of the debris and headed for a tree. The mother bear pounced and missed. The woodchuck climbed almost to the top of the tree, whistling in rage. The mother bear stretched up to her full height but she was still far below the branch where the woodchuck clung.

The male cub started up the trunk of

the tree. His mother was unable to climb it because she was too heavy for the tree and also because her front claws were straight, but the cub's claws were still curved. His mother woofed at him anxiously, in her low, coughing voice. When he was close to the woodchuck, he looked up. The animal stretched his head down toward the bear, his fierce teeth bared. He chattered his teeth together in fast clicking sounds, and hissed and growled. Alarmed, the cub backed down the tree and ran to the safety of his mother. The woodchuck already forgotten, she went back to the field and continued on her way.

The wind had shifted again, blowing into their faces and bringing a variety of smells. The mother bear stopped and sniffed, then quicked her pace to a fast lope. In a few minutes they came to a dead cow lying near a clump of wild larkspur. The larkspur, which is poisonous to cattle, had killed her, apparently not long before. The magpies had gathered, and a young coyote trotted off when he saw the three bears.

The mother bear sniffed at the carcass.

She would have preferred an animal that had been dead longer, but she was not going to pass up good meat when it was at hand. She began to eat, and the cubs joined her. The magpies flew up a little way, flapping their strong wings, but soon they settled down to eat too, not too close to the bears. After a while the coyote came back, and he too joined the feast.

They all ate steadily for some time. Then the coyote looked up and howled. His ears were tensed forward, and his yellow eyes peered across the open fields behind them. The mother bear stopped eating, looked at the coyote, and then turned to see what he saw.

A small object that was quickly getting bigger was headed toward them, bouncing across the broken land. And now the male cub tipped his head to one side; he could hear the strange noise the thing made, a roaring, sputtering noise.

The coyote tore off one more chunk of meat and trotted off to the shelter of the woods. Without seeming to hurry, the bear dug up a pile of dirt and buried what was left of the cow. But before she could finish, a jeep with two men in it roared toward them. She gathered up her cubs and shooed them toward the woods.

The female cub, more curious than frightened, broke away to get a better look. The mother bear bounded after her, shielding her from the men in the jeep. The male cub, left uprotected by the sudden move his mother had made, turned to look at the approaching jeep. His mother barked at him sharply, and he turned toward her. But the jeep stopped, and his curiosity made him look back once more.

One of the men rested the dull steel barrel of his gun on the top of the window and fired. The male cub felt a hot, stinging pain in the side of his jaw and in his shoulder. As he staggered from the impact of the shot, he tried to howl, but the bullet had chipped a piece of his jaw. Blood filled his mouth. He tried to run for his mother, but he stumbled and fell.

He heard a man's shout, and then he saw his mother galloping toward the jeep. The gun was fired again, but the shot went wild. The mother bear crashed against the side of the jeep with a force that dented in the metal. The man next to the driver screamed.

"Get out of here, Jerry! Get us out!"

The engine roared, and died. The driver's voice was a frightened yelp. "It's stalled!" Again there was a cranking sound as he tried to get the car started.

The big bear was standing on her hind legs, her front paws draped over the window. The man in the seat had slid down onto the floor. The cub could hear him moaning. The bear rocked the jeep, each rocking motion a little closer to tipping it over.

Then the engine roared, and the jeep got under way with a jerk that threw the mother bear off balance. She caught herself and came down hard on all fours, but when she started to gallop after the jeep, a bullet that whistled past her head changed her mind.

As the jeep bounced recklessly across the field, back toward where it had come from, the bear wheeled and came back to her cubs. She nuzzled the wounded cub, investigating his wound. The little bear staggered to his feet. His shoulder hurt,

but it was only a superficial wound. It was his jaw that gave him the most pain. His mother, standing between him and the disappearing jeep, gently urged him into the sheltering woods.

All the rest of the day they traveled up into the mountains, the mother bear stopping often so the little cub could rest. Whenever she stopped, she looked back down the trail, to make sure they were not being followed.

Late in the afternoon, she led them to a place where they sometimes slept. They stayed there for almost an hour, the little cub lying on his side and moaning softly. His mother and sister ate some huckleberries, but the cub couldn't move his jaw without great pain so he ate nothing. When his mother lay down beside him, he pushed against her, looking for comfort. She made low, soothing sounds to him, and finally he fell asleep for a short time.

It was already twilight when she gently nudged him awake and started up on the trail. Staggering with weakness, the little cub followed in her footprints.

5

The cub spent a restless night in the hollow, high up on the mountain where his mother had taken him. A summer snowstorm fell on them during the first hours of dawn, and the cool touch of the snow felt good to the feverish little bear. He was very hungry. He snuggled up to his mother to get some of her milk, which lately he had not bothered with because he had become interested in so many other kinds of food. The warm milk quieted the pangs of hunger, but even this much movement of his jaw hurt him so much that he finally rolled over on his side, whimpering.

All the next day, and the day after that, he lay in the hollow, only half aware of the coming and going of his mother and sister. His mother was never far away, and often she came to him, sniffing the healing wound on his shoulder, making low comforting sounds.

Toward noon on the fourth day he staggered to his feet to go with his mother and sister to the huckleberry patch. He couldn't open his mouth very far, but he was able now to eat some berries. Weak with hunger, he ate and ate and ate, until his face and chest were streaked with berry juice. Then he went to the stream nearby and drank from the icy water. He felt a little better. He even responded for a few minutes when his sister tried to play with him, but when she bumped against his head, he bawled with pain and ran away from her. She stood looking after him, puzzled.

Later he was eating again in the berry patch when he heard his mother's voice.

She was some distance behind him. As he turned to look at her, she reared up half-way, then dropped onto all fours again, with a loud roar of anger. The cub looked in the direction she was facing. Standing at the edge of the huckleberry bushes was an enormous male bear, a dark brown bear with big white patches on his chest. The cub had seen him before.

For a moment the two adult bears faced each other across the tangle of berry bushes. Then with a bellow the mother bear charged. The bear stood his ground for a moment, but just before she reached him, he turned his back on her and sauntered down the trail. She stood on her hind legs watching until he was out of sight.

In the late afternoon, a black bear with two cubs came to the berry patch to eat. The two sets of cubs eyed each other curiously, but the mother bears fed in their separate corners as if they were not even aware of each other.

For many days the Grizzly bears stayed high on the mountain, where man would have trouble surprising them. The gullies that creased the side of the mountain were slippery with granular summer snow, and the trails were over treacherous, sliding shale and through small, dense patches of wind-stunted trees and brush. Food was not as plentiful as it was below.

The mother bear never wandered far from the cubs, but early one morning, when she had been gone longer than usual, she came back with the partly decomposed carcass of a bull elk. After they had eaten, she buried it not far from their hollow. Each day she dug it out again for another feast, until it was gone.

The little bear's jaw was healing but he would always have a scar along the side of this muzzle, and he would never be able to open his mouth as wide as he once had. And sometimes, even with it nearly healed, a sudden sharp pain would make him bellow.

Never again that year did the bears venture down into the lowlands, though sometimes they went part-way down the mountain looking for food. As summer turned to Indian summer, they feasted on buffalo berries, raspberries, saskatoons, roots, nuts, and pinecones. Sometimes they discovered a horde of pine nuts that a ground squirrel had stored away for the winter. Once their mother took them to the shore of a lake nestled in a hollow of the mountain. The male cub crouched on her back and the female cub clung to her tail, as the mother bear swam the lake. On the far side they found a whole field of roots that they dug up and ate.

A few nights later the temperature dropped sharply, and the edges of the lake were skimmed with ice. Now the snow began to fall, drifting down in dry powdery flakes, sometimes from a sky that was still bright blue.

Late in October the mother bear led her cubs back to the den where they had been born. Although it was already cold, especially at night, she didn't move into the den right away. She worked hard, digging out the den to a larger size, and covering the floor with evergreen boughs and bark, grass, twigs, and leaves. The cubs romped in and out of the cave, getting in the way of their patient mother.

They were plump now and their coats

were glossy, but for several days they had been eating very little, and for the last few days before they entered the den for the winter, they ate nothing at all.

When a snow fell that was heavy enough to cover their footprints, the mother took her cubs into the den to stay. The falling and blowing snow almost at once erased any signs that they had been there, as it piled up on the dirt and twigs and debris that the mother bear had scooped out of the cave and left at the entrance.

The cubs circled around, and when their mother lay down, they snuggled up against her, already drowsy. Outside, a cold wind shrieked through the canyons, blowing the snow in great white clouds. But inside the den, the long winter sleep had begun.

Part II

1

A warm, gentle breeze melted the last of the snow that had filled the opening of the den. A little stream of water trickled into the den and touched the male cub's nose. He opened his eyes sleepily. His mother was already on her feet, sniffing the air at the entrance. His sister looked at him with sleep-dazed eyes. She looked different: bigger, with a thicker coat. He himself was bigger, almost 130 pounds now.

He followed his mother down the slope,

his sister trailing along after them, still unsteady with sleep. In a few minutes, all three of them were feasting on glacier lilies. They ate all day long, and then the mother led them further down the mountain to one of the hidden hollows they had used for a resting place the summer before.

A fine, warm rain fell. Almost as if she had forgotten how big her cubs had grown, the mother bear started to stand over them as she had often done during rainstorms when they were little. But they were too big for that now, and their thick new coats shed the rain as well as hers did.

They spent most of the next day searching for food, eating grass, roots, insects, anything they could find. Toward the end of the afternoon they reached the top of a long slope still covered with snow. The mother bear stood for a moment looking down the hill. Then she sat down, put her paws on her knees, gave herself a little push, and tobogganed down the steep hill. Just before she reached some big rocks at the bottom of the slope, she dragged one of her paws as a brake. Then she flipped over on her stomach and used all her claws to bring herself to a stop. She got up, shook herself, and looked back up the hill at the cubs.

The male cub sat down in the exact spot from which his mother had taken off, put his front paws on his knees as she had done, and hitched himself along until he too was speeding down the hill. His ability to brake to a stop was not as accurate as his mother's. Just before the bottom of the slope, he lost his balance and flailed wildly, landing in a heap at her feet. He got to his feet and started for the top of the hill again, just as his sister sped past him.

He capered and danced on the way up the hill, chasing his shadow on the snow. At the top, he tobogganed down again, this time coming to an expert stop, just short of a boulder. For more than an hour the cubs enjoyed their new game, while their mother went about the more serious business of finding food. Later, when they joined her, they found her eating the remains of a pronghorn that had perished during the winter. To their surprise, she snapped and growled at them when they tried to eat, too, but after a while she let them share. In the days that followed, she often wandered away from them, but she always came back. Each time she went out of their sight, however, the cubs bawled nervously and tried to run after her.

One day as they came down a steep trail at her heels, she stopped and reared up. The cubs skidded against her, surprised at her sudden stop. Before they had time to see what was happening, a man on a horse came around the bend in the trail. The man had a gun slung across the saddle, but he was too surprised to reach for it. The horse neighed in fear and tried to rear, slamming the man against the rocky wall on the inside of the trail.

The two cubs watched fearfully. The trail was narrow, with a long drop on the outside. Turning around would be easy for them, because they were still small enough, but for their mother and for the man on the horse, it would be difficult.

The big bear stood her ground, growling, and clicking her tooth, but she made no move to charge. The man, on his feet now, with his back to the rocky cliff, was struggling to control the terrified horse. The horse reared, slipped, and nearly fell off the trail, but the young man, sweating, straining on the reins, got him away from the dangerous edge and little by little began to back him down the trail. The man's broadbrim lay on the ground, trampled by the horse's hooves.

The mother bear stood where she was, waiting, for a long time. The cubs grew restless and tried to push past her, but she wouldn't let them go. Finally, long after the last sounds of the retreating horse and rider had faded away, she moved cautiously down the trail. As soon as she came to a place where the rock wall leveled out, she scrambled up to a ledge and moved at a fast, surefooted walk across the uneven ground until she had left the trail far behind.

For several weeks the mother bear kept her cubs far up in the mountains, at the edge of a small meadow that was bordered with snow and strewn with tiny flowers. At their backs, the mountains rose in a series of peaks, each higher than the one in front of it. Their snow-covered tops and snow-streaked sides were dazzling on days when the sun shone brightly and the sky was intensely blue.

The young male bear had lost weight after he came out from his winter sleep. All the bears grew thinner, because food was hard to find at first, and they gradually burned up the fat that had protected them through the winter. But for the young male, who was now a yearling, it was especially hard to get enough food, because of the gunshot wound that had left his jaw partly damaged. He couldn't chew with as much force as the other bears could. Sometimes his mother helped him, finding food that he could eat, and leaving it for him instead of eating it herself.

As the days grew warmer, finding food became easier. Sometimes the two yearlings spent a whole morning or part of a lazy afternoon just chasing grasshoppers, jumping clumsily and often falling. Occasionally their mother just sat and watched them, holding her back paws with her front paws and gently rocking back and forth.

One hot, humid day, the sky darkened in the early afternoon and storm clouds began to pile up over the peaks of the mountains. The bears were eating grass at the edge of the meadow, and the yearlings had begun to move further out into the open area.

A steady wind blew off the mountains. It lifted in its whistling sound, and lightning began to dance from peak to peak. The mother bear woofed a warning. But the young bears were enjoying the grass, and it had not begun to rain. She grunted at them more sharply, and from the long habit of obedience they trotted toward her.

The rain came in a sudden downpour; a great jagged shaft of lightning struck one of the rocky ledges not far behind them, and the thunder roared. The female yearling put her paws over her ears, trying to protect them from the noise. The bears stood huddled together just inside the first clump of trees.

Another bolt of lightning seemed to

split the curtain of dark rain. It lit up for an instant the figure of a man on a horse, at the far side of the meadow. In the same flash of lightning, he saw the bears. He lifted his gun and aimed. The shot, which the bears couldn't hear in the crash of thunder, went wild as the frightened horse reared. The bullet hit a stump some yards to the left of the male bear. He saw the chips of wood fly.

Both young bears huddled behind their mother for protection against the frightening combination of man, gun, thunder, and lightning. She moved back into the trees, and then angled off down a slope a short way. From there they could see the horseman. He was riding slowly across the open meadow, fighting his horse's urge to bolt. He rode to the middle of the meadow and dismounted, hobbling the horse. Then, with his gun ready, he walked slowly toward the spot where the bears had been.

The male bear shivered and pressed against his mother. She never took her eyes off the advancing hunter. Rain beat down through the trees, dripping off the bears' coats into the ground that had been hard a few minutes ago but was not soggy.

The whole sky seemed to shatter in a blinding flash of light and an ear-splitting roar of thunder. Both the younger bears pressed their paws to their ears, trying to keep out the pain of the enormous noise. The mother bear reared up on her hind legs, trying to see better.

The male yearling shook the water off his face and peered into the meadow. The horse lay still on the wet grass. The lightning had killed him. The man too was on the ground, knocked down by the force of the lightning. Slowly he got to his feet and looked back at his horse. He hesitated, then ran unsteadily to the dead animal, bent over him, and removed the saddle. Carrying it, the man walked fast, almost running, to the downhill side of the meadow. His gun lay where it had fallen in the grass.

The bears stayed perfectly still long after the man was out of sight. At last, when the storm moved on the south, they ventured out and approached the horse.

2

One fine summer morning the mother bear took her young bears fishing. The summer before, they had stood on the banks and watched her fish, eating with delight whatever she threw to them. But now they had to learn to fish for themselves, because very soon the mother bear would leave her cubs to go off on her own.

She led them down the steep side of the mountain to a spot where a mountain-fed stream joined another slower stream. It was a shady place, with tall pines along the banks, sometimes leaning far out over the water. In a few places the trees had fallen into the stream, making natural bridges for the bears. The mother bear stopped at a place where there was a gravel bar reaching halfway across the river.

The young bears wanted to splash into the water right away, but crossly she stopped them. They would drive the fish away.

The yearlings sat down obediently on the bank to watch her, as the big bear stepped out carefully on a log that hardly looked big enough to hold her. She balanced gracefully, in spite of her size, her four feet close together. From her perch, she peered down intently into the riffle in the water below her.

For a long time she didn't move. The cubs wriggled impatiently, but they sat where they were, watching. Then, so quickly that they could hardly see it happen, their mother thrust her nose into the slow swirl of the water and came up with a rainbow trout in her mouth. With the fish in her jaws she turned and came to the bank where the cubs were. They waited, quivering with excitement, while she delicately stripped the flesh from the bones. The male cub tried to grab a piece of the fish, but his mother growled at him and drove him away.

The cubs watched hungrily while she ate the fish. As she went back to the log to try again, a magpie dove down to investigate the bones. Hungry and annoyed, the male yearling rushed him, and the bird soared up again in a flash of black and white feathers.

When the mother bear looked back at him, the male took it as an invitation. Carefully he moved out on the log behind his mother. She made no move to drive him off. Encouraged, the female yearling ventured out on a log of her own. All three of them stared at the water.

The mother bear caught another fish in her mouth and tossed it up on the bank. This time the yearling was more interested in catching one of his own than in begging for hers. Imitating her in every way, he waited for his own fish.

Just below the surface of the sun-streaked water, he saw the flick of a tail. He thrust his head into the water, as his mother had done, trying to seize the quick fish in his jaws. But he lost his balance and slipped into the water with a great splash. He felt the sharp slap of the fish against the side of his head, but before he could catch it, it was gone.

He peered all around the pool, but he could see no fish. He waded out of the water and shook himself. His sister, on her own log, went on staring at the water, but his mother went to the bank and again ate the fish she had caught. Then she moved upstream, to get away from the water that had been roiled and disturbed by her cub's sudden falling in. She looked at one little backwater eddy, and then went on still further, the cubs trailing her.

The place where she finally stopped was a wider and deeper place in the stream. A logjam made a deep, slowly swirling pool, but the main part of the stream was faster than below.

The male chose his own log this time

and perched on it as his mother did on hers, digging in his claws so he wouldn't slip. Within a minute or two, the old bear had snatched a fish from the water, and the spray thrown up struck the yearling unexpectedly in the face. Startled, he slipped again, and sat down with a wet plop in water almost up to his ears.

Patiently the mother bear again sought out another fishing hole where the fish would not have been frightened off by her clumsy cub. Each time they stopped, the female cub found a log for herself and imitated her mother, but although she had not fallen in, she hadn't caught a fish either. Once or twice she batted at the water, but there was either no fish there or it was too fast for her.

The mother bear accumulated a pile of fish, and, not taking time to eat them, she heaped twigs and leaves over them for a later meal. Every now and then the male rushed to the pile of fish to drive off hungry crows. But most of the time he stood on his chosen log, peering into the rushing water on his right, and then into the still pool on his left. As he stood there in bright sunlight, his silver-tipped coat, with its light guard hairs over the darker undercoat, seemed almost white, especially on the hump just back of his shoulders.

Finally, like a flash, he plunged his head into the pool, and this time he came up with a fish. It wasn't a very big one, but it was a trout. He took it to the shore, near where his mother was fishing, and proudly threw it down on the ground for her to admire. She looked at it, came ashore and sniffed at it, but she made no move to eat it. This was the yearling's fish.

In his haste to enjoy his catch, the yearling gulped it down in one big bite. He choked and coughed, and put his paw inside his mouth. In a minute he felt better, and he went back to his log to fish some more.

All the rest of the day the three bears fished. The young female finally caught two small trout. The male, sure of himself once he had caught the first, caught half a dozen more. Some they ate, and some they buried for a later meal.

Just before dark they went to a resting place that they had often used the summer before. But they stopped short. It was occupied.

A big male bear stood there watching them. His summer-ragged coat was chocolate brown, and he had two yellow stripes from his shoulders to his haunches.

The yearling growled in his throat and waited for his mother to drive the intruder out. But she did nothing. For a minute she just stood there, looking at the big male. Then she turned and lumbered out of the thicket to another place farther down the trail. There they bedded down for the night, but the yearling slept badly, uneasy about having the big stranger so near.

When he awoke, just as the sky was beginning to show streaks of silver light, he found that his mother had gone.

3

He waited a few minutes, expecting her to come back from some little excursion for food. But she didn't come. The sky grew lighter, and the sun balanced like a fiery circle on a distant mountain peak. He nudged his sister awake, and at once she began to whimper for her mother.

Together they explored the whole area, expecting any minute to come across their mother, digging up a pine squirrel or enjoying a meal of chokecherries. But she was nowhere to be found. Both yearlings were badly frightened. The female began to bawl louder and louder, until her brother gave her a sharp cuff. Then they wrestled together for a few minutes, almost forgetting what the trouble was.

All morning they looked for their mother, not even stopping to eat. But in the afternoon hunger overcame them, and they went to the chokecherry trees to feast on the tart berries.

The young silvertip male saw what looked to him like a ground squirrel colony. Digging frantically, as he had so often watched his mother do, he finally laid bare some of the burrows, but they were deserted. He pounced on a few pine nuts that he found in one of the burrows, but they were not plentiful enough to make a meal.

Overcome again with longing for his mother, and especially with a feeling of not being safe without her, he loped back to the resting place. But she was not there. He coughed impatiently at his sister, who kept close to his heels, but although she moved away for a minute, she was soon back, whimpering in a desolate way.

He tried to think where his mother might be. He found it hard to remember where she usually took them. In a sudden rage of frustration, he attacked a clump of a juniper and clawed at it until it was in shreds, the pungent juniper smell filling the air.

Hearing a sound on the trail, he rolled his lips back and woofed in a hoarse voice. The female raced out to the trail, expecting to see her mother. But in an instant she was back. Together they peered through the bushes as a mother skunk and her three offspring strolled in a leisurely way along the trail, stopping here and there to rest. The skunk, small though she was, was one animal the bears knew enough not to bother. They waited in respectful stillness until the little family had paraded by.

When darkness came and the mother bear had not returned, the silvertip and his sister settled down uneasily for the night.

In the morning they left their resting place and went back along the trail, looking everywhere. It was almost noon when the young female let out a loud, happy woof, and bounded off the trail toward a small clearing. The silvertip followed his sister. In the middle of the opening stood their mother. She looked at them for a moment, and then as they raced up to her, she jerked away. Still they tried to tumble over her feet and rub up against her. Angrily she swatted at the male with her big paw. It wasn't a hard blow, but it was enough to send him sprawling. He bawled in pain and surprise. Immediately his sister also was cuffed out of the way. The mother turned her back on them and began to walk away.

Unable to believe it, both bears tried again to follow her, but they got the same reception, and this time the whack on the silvertip's ear really hurt. He sat on the ground, his paw against his ear, moaning in pain and distress.

For a while they stayed behind their mother, at a safe distance, but finally she turned and charged them. They fled, then, bawling loudly.

Back in the glade where they had found her, they sat down and looked at each

other. Neither of them understood what was happening. And they didn't know what to do.

Because it was the last place they had seen her, they stayed in that area for a long time. The silvertip made a bed of pine boughs and pine needles, and they slept there that night.

In the morning the male lumbered to his feet, awakened by a sound. The big bear with the lemon-colored stripes stood looking at him. The young bear growled uneasily but he didn't give in to the impulse to run. In a few minutes the big bear turned and crashed off through the brush. Later in the day the two young bears saw the bear again, this time with their mother. The two were feeding side by side.

As the two young bears watched from a safe distance, the big bears stopped eating and began to wrestle and cuff each other like a pair of cubs. Although the yearlings longed for their mother, they knew better than to interrupt her again. At last they turned and went back to their bed in the hollow, where they felt a little safer than anywhere else.

In the next two weeks they saw their mother and the yellow-striped bear several times, but after that, whenever they saw their mother, she was alone, and if she saw them, she angrily chased them away. In the spring she would have new cubs; it was time for the yearlings to look after themselves. But for a long time they continued to mourn for their mother, and to feel frightened of every unexpected noise or scent.

4

The brother and sister stayed close to each other all the time, finding some feeling of safety in being together. They were learning to forage for food with the same energy that their mother had used.

One afternoon, when the first chill touch of fall had already reached the high elevations, the two yearlings came to a lake where they sometimes found a few small fish near the shore. The water in the lake was a deep green, and it was very deep and cold.

For a little while they looked for fish without any luck, moving finally along the shore to a clump of serviceberry bushes. Using their paws to break off branches, they scooped the berries into their mouths.

At the sound of splash in the lake, they turned to look. Out in the middle of the lake, swimming toward them, was a bull moose, only his dark wet head and his antlers visible. The huge antlers were hung with ragged velvet. Not noticing the bears, he swam to shore only a few yards from them and stood rubbing his antlers against a tree. Then he stood for a moment with his head lifted, scenting the wind, and plunged back into the lake. His head kept disappearing altogether as he ducked down, looking for the water plant that he liked to eat.

The bears stayed in their hiding place, afraid he would notice them if they moved away. At most times of the year a moose wouldn't pay any attention to them, but this was mating season and instinct told them to keep out of the way.

They stayed in the bushes for some

time, until the moose showed signs of heading for the opposite shore. Then just as they were about to leave, they heard a sharp report. It was a faint sound, as if it came from far away. Although the young bear could not remember what it was, he knew he had heard it before and it made him uneasy. But he almost forgot his nervousness in the curiosity about the moose. Almost together with the sound of the report, the head of the moose jerked violently to one side. Now he was struggling in the water, and all around him the green lake was turning red. For a long time he thrashed in the water. Then he lay still, floating half submerged.

The bears watched closely. In a few minutes the moose was close to shore, his huge body lifting and falling on the gentle waves. The animal brushed against the sandy edge of shore, drifted a little way out, and was carried back in again. There was no sound anywhere.

The two bears came out of their shelter and stepped cautiously along the beach toward the moose. Ever since their mother had gone, they had lived almost

entirely on roots, berries, and grass. Now they could smell the moose, and it made them very hungry.

The young bear's sister stopped some distance from the moose, as if she were afraid to go closer, but the silvertip went directly to the dead animal. A few feet away he stopped and waited. Nothing happened. He walked into the water and seized the moose by the loose skin on his neck. Instantly there was a tremendous commotion, as the mortally wounded moose roused himself for one last effort to survive. He half rolled, to get away from the bear's teeth, and he struck out with his sharp hoof. The hoof caught the bear in the side of the head. If the moose had not been so stricken, the blow would have killed the bear, but it was a feeble slash that hurt but did no serious damage.

It didn't occur to the young bear now to abandon the fight. He got to his feet and charged the moose, clacking his teeth. The moose struggled to get to his feet, but he couldn't get up. Blood streamed from the bullet wound in his chest, and his eyes were glazed. Still, he thrashed feebly in the few inches of water, trying to aim another blow at the bear's head.

But then he stopped moving, and in seconds he was dead. The two bears now combined their strength, trying to pull the 1,400-pound animal onto the beach. In a few minutes they had the forequarters beached, and the momentum of the gently lapping water on the shoreline was helping them get the big creature onto dry land. They worked hard, hunger urging them on. They would eat well tonight, and they would be able to bury enough meat for many more meals.

From the thickly wooded hillside above them, a voice called out; a voice that the young bear dimly remembered having heard before.

"Hey, Pop, you got it! You nailed him! Pop, over here, I *told* you you was on the wrong trail. . . ."

A voice farther away answered, a loud, triumphant yell. "Got him, did I?"

"Hurry up, Pop. There's two Grizzlies workin' at it . . ."

"Get 'em!" The older voice was closer now, sounding out of breath. "We'll get us a bear too."

But already the two bears had bolted for the woods. They found a thicket so dense they could hardly force their way into it. Its many branches scratched and tore at their fur, but it made good cover. They halted there, and the voices of the two men were fainter.

"Where's them Grizzlies?"

"They took off. Can't expect 'em to stand around and wait for you. Look at the rack on that moose, Pop. Bet you that's mighty near a 5-foot spread."

"Why didn't you get a shot at them bears?"

"Pop, forget the bears, will you? We got enough to do, dressing out this moose. Cripes, we got enough meat here to take us right through the winter."

For a long time the men worked, dressing out the moose and removing the rack. All that time the bears never moved. When the men were finally ready to move the moose, the older man said, "You go get the packhorses now. And mind they don't spook. If they smell bear . . ."

"All right," the boy said. "But don't get no ideas about going off after the bear, will you, Pop? You stay right here, OK?"

"You just do as you're told," the man said sharply. "You ain't big enough yet to give me orders."

"Pa, I just . . ."

"Get along."

The bears heard the boy go off, whistling, crashing through the brush. In a few minutes the smell of man grew much stronger. The silvertip wrinkled his nose and pulled back his lip. He stood tense, ready to charge. But the man went on by their hiding place, and although he made a wide circuit of the area around the beach, he didn't discover them.

After some time the boy came back with two packhorses, and they loaded the meat onto the animals. Both horses were uneasy; they nickered and looked around them with wild, rolling eyes.

"Them bears is around here some place," the man said. "I'm coming back tomorrow to take a look."

"They'll be long gone."

"Maybe so, maybe not." He gave one of the horses a hard slap with the palm of his hand. "Git along."

The bears listened until they could hear nothing more, and until the scent of the men was gone. Even then, they waited a while longer. Then they came out of their thicket, and, doing as their mother would have done, they started the long climb toward the greater safety of high rimrock and canyon.

5

The bears stayed together for the rest of the summer, huddling close at night in one of the two or three bedding-down places they had made for themselves high in the hills and looking for food together during the day. But sometimes they growled and snapped at each other, and once or twice the silvertip went off by himself, trying to leave his sister behind. One morning when she had found and killed a big jackrabbit, she drove her brother away from the meal.

Early in the autumn, the silvertip set out in the early morning for the stream where their mother had taught them to fish. His sister followed him, but she stayed some distance behind him, and they paid no attention to each other.

They fished and feasted until the hot midmorning sun drove them into the woods to rest. When they came back, in the late afternoon, two other bears were fishing in the stream, each concentrating on his own pool, paying no attention to the other. One of them was the dark brown bear with white patches on his chest, whom the young bears had seen twice before. He was by far the biggest bear they had ever seen. The silvertip found a place to fish that was a comfortable distance from him.

There were so many kokanee salmon spawning in the stream that not only the bears but other creatures came, too, to join in the harvest of fish. Just above the silvertip, where the stream widened and flowed through an area that was more open, there were almost two hundred bald eagles, attracted from many parts of the country by the feast of salmon. The fish, which had returned to the river where they were born four years before, spawned and then died, completing their part of the mysterious life cycle that brought them back many miles, from the ocean where they had lived out most of their lifetime.

The fish, which were about a foot long, clotted the surface of the river, and there was a strong smell of decaying fish everywhere. The young male bear could also faintly detect a man smell and it made him uneasy, although he was unable to see the forest ranger, some distance away, who stood on a bridge made of saplings and watched the eagles through his binoculars.

The bear kept his distance, too, from the huge white-capped eagles: many of them were as much as 6 feet from wingtip to wingtip. They had come from Canada as well as from many parts of the western states, knowing somehow that the salmon would be there.

Otters dove into the water after fish, and mink came slinking along the shore looking for their share. Gulls were interspersed with the eagles, diving with dazzling speed, right on target, then screaming and diving again. On a sandbar two great blue herons picked at remains that had been cast up there by other creatures. Sometimes a fox trotted up to see what was going on, and once a bobcat materialized out of nowhere with a ruffled grouse in his mouth. In another instant he was gone.

The bears stayed at this stream, where food was so plentiful, for another week, eating almost constantly except for their naps. On the fourth day the eagles began to leave. First about half of them left; a day later only about 85 were there. And at the end of the week, all were gone. Along the shore and on the gravel bars, the remains of the salmon rotted and fell apart.

Finally the bears left, for once so full of food that they were able to go for at least a few hours without hunting for more. But winter was in the air, and by the next day they were foraging again, seeking out a squirrel's hoard of pine nuts, or, with luck, the squirrel himself. They ate the last of the berries, and chewed on sedge, and dug up roots.

Gradually they worked their way back to the den where they had been born, but when they got there, they found their mother there. She growled at them warningly, and when the male did not go away at once, she made a quick charge, as if to attack him.

Leading his sister, the young bear headed off in a new direction, to an area they had never been before. That night they went about 30 miles, stopping when they came to woods where the trees had been bent by the constant wind so that they looked as if they were all bowing. He dug around there until he found the kind of place he wanted, a hollowed-out hole between the roots of two trees.

The next morning they began to dig out the hollow so it would be big enough for them both. They worked hard, and the area around the trees was soon piled up with loose dirt, bark, twigs, and pine needles.

Frequently through the day they

stopped work to find food, although they were eating less and less now, as the time came closer for their winter sleep.

As they had seen their mother do, they lined the floor of the den with boughs and leaves, to make it comfortable. Every now and then, the young silvertip went to the edge of the cliff, stood on his hind legs, and tried to see down the long, irregular jumble of gullies, canyons, cliffs, and streams. He seemed to be looking for something in particular.

At twilight one evening, shortly before he settled down for the night, he went again to the edge of the cliff and looked down the sweep of the mountains. This time he saw what he had been looking for. A man on horseback rode slowly down the bear trail far below him, and in a few seconds another, smaller rider came into view, following the first. They would not have seen the bear if they had looked up, because he stood in the shelter of the trees, but he watched them for a long time without moving, until at last they disappeared.

That night it snowed, and the young

bear nudged his sister toward the den. It was time for the winter sleep. After she had settled down, he went out again for one last look around. The snow was falling in big, swirling flakes, and already it had covered up the debris that had been dug out of the cave. Soon the snow would make a door for the cave. He wagged his head slowly from side to side, searching for smells. Satisfied at last, he went back into the cave, circled around twice, and settled down.

Part III

1

Twice during the long winter, the silver-tip woke and went outside the den. He paced up and down for about 60 feet, making a path in the crusty snow. When he got to the end of his route, he reared up each time and looked in all directions. The second time he came out, in the middle of March, he lay down for about an hour in the morning sunshine. The warm sun made him even sleepier than he had been when he came out of his den. His head drooped and drooped, until he caught himself with a jerk; then it drooped again. He wouldn't let himself go to sleep while he was outside, but it was hard to stay awake and finally he lumbered to his feet and went back into the den. His sister opened her eyes, then went back to sleep again almost at once.

One more time the silvertip woke, but didn't come out of his den. An early spring thaw had melted the top snow, and he could hear the water dripping steadily outside. There was a little puddle of snow water at the entrance, but the den was angled so that the water didn't flood in. He lay quietly listening to the slow drip of the water as the snow melted on the trees. In the distance he heard the dull boom of an avalanche. On the other side of the mountain, the bear with the yellow stripes came out of his den to escape the water that flooded it. Almost as soon as he came out, he was shot dead by the man who hated Grizzlies. The silvertip heard the shot; he lifted his head, tense, his rounded ears listening, his nose twitching. But all was still, and after a while, he went back to sleep.

When he finally ended his winter's sleep, he found that his sister had already left the den. He got up and lumbered out into the warm spring sunshine. His sister was some distance away, digging for roots. He stood up on his hind legs and investigated the surroundings. He was a big two-year-old now, almost 250 pounds of fat and muscle, with a rich, thick coat. He would keep on growing for another 5 years, until he reached 600 or 700 pounds, but he was already a big bear for his age. When he came near his sister, she looked small beside him.

They both ate hungrily, but they didn't stay as close together as they had before. After about a week, the female wandered off into the woods, and the silvertip didn't go after her. They would see each other now and again, in the years ahead, but they would pay no more attention to each other than to a stranger. Except for the mother bear and her young cubs, the adult Grizzly keeps no ties of friend or family.

And so the young bear was on his own. He ate steadily, and scratched and rubbed against trees until his coat was scraggly and patchy. And always he kept alert for the sound or the smell of a man with a gun. Sometimes he dug furiously for an hour to catch one small ground squirrel that was devoured in a second. Sometimes he tried the streams again, for whatever small fish he could catch at that time of year, but they were tiny and swift and hard to grab. He spent much energy in pursuit of food he didn't catch. But there were always the early flowers, the grass, the roots.

His favorite resting place was a shady, scooped-out place at the foot of a giant ponderosa, just off the trail that he generally followed up and down the mountain. One afternoon in midsummer he rose from a nap, stretched his muscles, and ambled out to still another trail that he had made. It was late afternoon, and time to look for some food. He stood on the trail, his huge front feet with their long, rigid claws, planted in the same prints that he always made. He wondered whether to go up the trail or down. Yesterday he had caught a snake partway

down the mountain. He turned in that direction.

Just as he turned, with a light evening wind at his back, a young man loomed up almost directly in front of him. The bear stopped and growled low in his throat. The young man stopped short too. He had a gun in his hand, but he made no move to use it. For a long moment they stared at each other.

Then the young man started to talk, in a low, intense voice, as if he were very anxious for the bear to understand him. "Look, bear, get out of here right now. I mean, you git, Mister Bear. My pa is coming up the trail behind me, and if there's one thing in the world he loves to do, it's kill a Grizzly. I don't mean you no harm, bear. I don't like killing things. I go along with my pa because he raises such a row if I don't. But I like animals. I like you, bear." He paused and took a long breath. "I don't know if you're gettin' ready to kill me or not. They say it don't even hurt when you first get bit by a bear; they say you don't hardly feel it. But I'd give a whole lot not to find out."

He paused again, and waited. "Why don't you just skedaddle out of here now, before my father comes. He's a mean man with a bear, he really is. And he's an awful good shot. I'd like to run, if you want to know. I'd like to run out of here like I never run before. I don't think I'd hardly even touch the ground. But I know you can run a whole lot faster than I can, so I ain't going to do it. If you kill me, bear, you got to do it face to face." He stopped talking.

The bear didn't move.

Below them, still some distance away, a voice called out. "Where are you at, Boy? I found bear sign all over this trail. I'm going to get me another bear today, sure as the Lord."

The young man didn't answer.

They both heard the crack of twigs as the older man made his way up the trail. At last the silvertip swung halfway around and went into the woods. He moved into a shadow stand of trees and brush, where it would be hard to get a clear shot at him, and he turned and waited.

He heard the father's voice.

"I been yelling at you. Why didn't you sing out?"

"I knew you was coming up the trail. You'd find me. And we're never going to catch anything if we advertise ourselves all over the hills."

The father gave a dry little laugh. "By gum, I believe you're learnin'. You may amount to something one of these days after all. Come on, let's work our way up the trail. There's a bear been using this hill regular, and lately."

"All right, Pop."

The bear heard them climbing the hill. Now, when they were upwind of him, their scent was very strong and unpleasant in his nose. He stayed where he was until darkness came. Then he started off across the mountains, and he didn't stop until noon of the next day.

2

The silvertip found a comfortable new bedding ground in the woods near a wide stream that poured in a froth of white water over the rocks in its way. Far off, he could hear a steady sound like thunder that never stopped. At first it made him anxious, and he considered moving farther up into the hills, but after a few days, his curiosity was too much for him.

Moving like a bulky shadow through the woods, he approached the place of thunder. The sound grew louder and louder as he came closer, and the stream rushed along with increasing speed. Even several feet away from it, he could feel the spray on his face.

He stopped to chew on the bark of a cottonwood tree and to consider the situation. He had been sniffing the air constantly, but there was nothing to alarm him. He finished off the cottonwood bark with great mouthfuls of the browse that grew along the bank of the river. Then he moved on again, toward the thunder.

The sound hurt his ears. He stood up on his hind legs but still couldn't see what was making it. It all made him very uneasy, but he was too curious to go away. He swung off a little to the left of the stream and went ahead at a cautious walk.

At the edge of a clearing he saw what was making all the noise. On the shore of a vast lake, a dam stretched almost further than he could see, and water from the lake fell over it in a wide silver sheet. Far below, at the bottom of the dam, the water churned in great whirlpools, breaking over rocks in the stream bed, hurling logs and branches into the air or catching them in dizzying circles. The spray, flung up from the tumult of water, caught the sun and turned all colors of the rainbow.

The bear had seen waterfalls, but he had never seen anything like this. To his dim eyes the lake that poured its water over the dam seemed to go on forever. He couldn't see the opposite shore nor the beginning of the lake. He stood and looked at it all for a long time, remembering to search the dense forest behind him and the shoreline above and below him for any signs of man. Once a deer leaped through the brush, further up the lake shore, but the bear paid no attention to him.

After a while he picked his way carefully down the steep path that led to the bottom of the dam. The air was cool and pleasant and the spray soaked into his coat. Except for the noise, it was a good place to be on a hot day. The ground was wet, and his big paws made muddy tracks. His claws had been worn down some by all the digging he had done since he got out of his winter den, but they were still long and each one left its mark in the ground.

At the foot of the falls he stood upright, his paws covering his ears, and let the spray soak him. He watched a big log spin in a whirlpool, then upend itself and hurtle on down the river.

The noise was too much for him, and he felt exposed, standing there by the noisy water, where he couldn't hear anything else or smell anything except the water. He lumbered on down beside the river. In places, the ground was covered with heaps of debris, and stumps stuck up out of muddy soil, where trees had been felled. He made a quick search of some of the debris, but there was nothing there to eat; it was just dead wood and leaves.

He followed a stream that branched off the main river, and in a few minutes he came to a slanted wooden weir that was built between cement walls on either side of the stream. He smelled fish. He stopped and peered into the shallow water. On the upstream side of the barrier some dead whitefish floated, bumping against the wooden structure that had prevented them from swimming downstream. The bear ate them all. He waded into the cold water and found other fish, smaller ones, and he ate them. He ate for a long time, undisturbed.

On his way back to his resting place, he crossed a railroad track, a new track that had been cut through the forest, again with stumps and trash left on both sides. He walked down the track a little way, sniffing at the steel rails. Once he tried to bite a rail, but it tasted bad and hurt his jaw. Along the way he came upon a deer that had been struck and killed by a train. He ate what he wanted and carefully buried the rest.

In later days he went back for the rest of the deer, although some of it had been dug up and stolen by coyotes. And often he returned to the barrier that destroyed the fish. Occasionally he found another bear there, but the two fed quietly, paying no attention to each other.

One day as he stepped out of the woods, he woofed in surprise. A man in a dark green uniform was bending over the water on the downstream side of the

weir, dumping tiny fish from a bucket into the water. He looked up at the bear.

"Woof yourself," he said, "and good morning to you." He picked up another bucket and carefully poured it into the water. "In case you're curious, Mr. Bruin, I'm stocking the stream with trout to make the fishermen happy. Not you, my friend; human fishermen. You can eat the trash fish on the other side. Is it a deal?" He stood up in a slow, easy motion and faced the bear.

For some reason the bear didn't feel afraid of this man, although he watched him carefully.

"You've got it made here, old boy. Your own private fish market. But you leave my fingerlings alone, you hear?" He stacked his buckets and walked away.

3

Other bears, and other animals and birds, discovered the feast of fish at the new wooden weir, and often when the silvertip went there for a meal, he had company.

Coming back one evening, well fed and content, with fish scales still clinging to his face, he heard a commotion in the woods ahead of him. The smell on the wind told him it was bear.

He approached cautiously until he was close enough to see. A golden brown female, rather small, was feeding on an anthill, seeming to pay no attention to two males who faced each other, growling and clacking their teeth. One of the males was the old pinto, with the white marks on his chest. The other, a smaller one, was a bald-faced Grizzly, with light blond fur on his face and the top of his head, darker fur starting at his hump and on the rest of his body. He was dish-faced, with a caved-in looking profile.

The silvertip had no interest in the female; it would be at least another year, perhaps two or three, before he was ready to mate. But he was curious about the male bears. He stayed concealed in a thicket, watching.

Both bears stood with their heads low, their ears cocked forward, woofing and growling louder and louder. Suddenly the bald-faced bear lunged forward and sank his teeth into the pinto's shoulder. The force of his rush knocked them both off their feet, but the pinto tore himself loose and reared up on his hind legs. He struck out at the bald-face with his enormous paw. Bleeding from the raking claws, the bald-face too reared up on his hind legs.

The two faced each other, their mouths open, their deadly teeth ready to bite. In a motion so fast that it was impossible to tell who moved first, they charged each other. The bald-face sank his teeth into the pinto's throat, but the pinto struck him another tearing blow and got loose. Both bears were bleeding badly, and both were roaring at the top of their voices.

The female, the object of all this fighting, glanced at them and moved farther away.

The pinto ripped fur from the neck of the bald-face, and in a second lunge got hold of his ear. The bald-face shook himself with all his strength. He got loose, and suddenly he turned away. As soon as the smaller bear made this sign of submission, the pinto stopped his attack. Bleeding and torn, the bald-faced Grizzly staggered off, out of sight.

The pinto, his sides heaving, stood still for a moment on the blood-soaked, fur-strewn ground. Then he moved closer to the female and began to feed on roots, as if nothing had happened.

But as the young silvertip started to go

on up the trail, the pinto heard him, and turning like lightning he charged him. With a yip of fear, the young bear broke into a gallop. He felt the sharp tearing of long claws on his haunch, but then the pinto turned back and let him go. The silvertip kept on galloping until he was safely out of range.

For a long time he avoided that trail. Instead, he went higher up into the mountains in his endless search for food.

Early one morning he sat looking up at the almost sheer rock wall above him. A mountain goat, a bearded nanny, leaped up the face of the rock to a narrow ledge. Her kid, whom the bear hadn't even seen, sailed through the air after his mother, and the two rolled on their backs, taking a dust bath. Their thick winter coats were almost gone, with only a few ragged-looking patches left.

After their bath, they stood chewing their cud, gazing off into the miles of space beyond them. The bear watched them for a long time. He would have very much liked a mountain goat for a meal, but he knew better than to try chasing them. Earlier in the spring he had seen them feeding on green grass at lower levels, and once he had been foolish enough to try to catch one. The goat had leaped straight up the nearest cliff, pulling himself up, finding toeholds in what looked like smooth rock face.

The bear went back to his resting place now, still hungry. But some time later a heavy rain started that lasted for several days. Again he was near the mountain goats' area, but the goats, who hated rain, had found caves or sheltering brush in which to wait out the storm.

The bear stayed where the trees would partly protect him from the rain. Once he caught a snow-shoe rabbit that leaped off the trail almost on top of the bear's front paws. And he ate bark from some of the trees. But it was hard to find food in the blinding rain, and he was getting very hungry.

Toward dawn of the third day of rain, he was startled by a dull roar, like thunder but lasting much longer than thunder. Shaking his head to get the water off his face, he tried to see what had happened, but it was still dark and the rain made it seem like pitch black night. He gave up and settled down again under the trees, where the rain dripped slowly and steadily through the wet branches.

In the morning the rain turned to a series of quick, gusty showers. The air was cool and fresh, and the storm clouds streamed off to the east in long, foggy strips, letting pale sunshine through.

The bear set out to see what changes the storm had made. After some searching he discovered the source of the long thunder he had heard the night before. There had been a rockslide. Torn-up trees, brush, gravel, and small rocks spread out in a wide area of debris at the bottom of a cliff. And half buried in the debris was a mountain goat, killed in the avalanche that had caught him on his precipice.

The bear ate for a long time, and when he had had enough, he dug a shallow hole and rolled the rest of the carcass into it. Digging with great energy, he buried it under a pile of dirt, rocks, moss, and twigs. He brought in torn-up plants and branches of trees from outside the avalanche area, and heaped these onto the hiding place too, until he had built up a mound 3 or 4 feet high. Then, satisfied, he went on his way.

4

Late in August the silvertip discovered that he was being stalked. For three days in a row he saw the man and his son, whom he had seen several times before. The son carried no gun. Instead, he had a camera, and from time to time he stopped to take pictures, once of a golden eagle circling above a canyon, once of mountain sheep, and once of a black bear cub in a tree some distance down the trail.

His father carried the gun. When he saw the cub, he lifted it and aimed, but his son knocked his arm and the shot went wild. The cub scampered down the tree and disappeared.

"What'd you have to go and do that for?" The father was angry.

"It's just a baby," the boy said. "Anyway, it wasn't a Grizzly. It's Grizzlies you're after, ain't it?"

"I'm after bear," the man said. "And don't you do a fool thing like that again. I don't know what I let you come up here with me for. You're just in my way."

The young man sighted through the scope on his camera, aiming it down at the river that plunged over the rocks far below them. "I figure sometimes I can talk you out of killing everything you see."

"You can't talk me out of nothing. I don't know what's got into you. When you was a young kid, you brought home your deer."

"And I always wished I hadn't done it. I like animals. I don't like 'em dead."

The man started up the trail again, grumbling.

On the first day he had found the place

where the silvertip usually rested, and he had lingered for a long time nearby, hidden in the woods. But the silvertip, some distance away, watched the watcher. And when night came, he found a new place to rest.

On the second day, the man carefully examined the old resting place and decided that the bear had left it. "He smelled us," he said to his son. "He's moved on." And he too moved on, climbing slowly, examining the trail every inch of the way for signs of the bear. It was a hot, sultry day, and the climb was steep, the trail narrow. The bear heard him coming. He stepped off the trail himself, and waited for the man to pass him.

The man climbed laboriously up the steep trail, passing not 10 feet from the Grizzly. In a few minutes the son came along. He stopped just beyond the place where the bear was hidden and took a picture of a starry white trillium that grew out of the hillside.

When the young man had gone on, the bear fell into the little procession, following the two men just far enough behind to keep out of sight. He followed them to the top of the mountain and partway down the other side.

He was getting tired of the game and was about to give it up when he heard two shots in quick succession, followed by a shout, and then the roar of a bear.

Alarmed, the silvertip hurried into the concealing trees and stood very still, his head lowered, ready to attack if he had to.

The young man came up the trail, almost running, gravel flying out from under his boots. He had his father's gun in his hand. His father came right behind him, almost choking with rage.

"I *had* that bear. You grabbed my gun . . ."

The son slowed up and turned his head. "You trying to get us both killed?"

"I had him cornered. He'd no way to turn around. When I get you home . . ." He made a grab for the gun, but the young man ran on up the trail.

Much later the silvertip ventured down the hill a way. There was no bear in sight, but in a narrow canyon that led to an open field, there was blood on the ground and patches of dark and white fur clinging to the rocks on both sides of the canyon. There was not enough room in the canyon for a big bear to have turned around; he would have had to back out. Even the silvertip would have had to go on through the canyon once he started in.

Instead he circled it and picked up the trail of blood on the other end. He saw the big, long-clawed prints of a Grizzly around the edge of the field. In a few minutes the blood stopped. The silvertip turned back. He had no wish to run into the big pinto bear, especially if he had been wounded.

The next day, the man and his son returned. Again the silvertip followed them. He saw them hesitate at the canyon.

"I ain't going in there," the younger man said. "That bear could be waiting for us on the other end, and he is an awful big bear."

His father said, "You're not only a big fool, Georgie, you're a coward."

"I probably saved your life yesterday, Pa. You couldn't kill that big bear just shooting at his rear end. He'd have got himself turned around in a minute and he'd have killed you for sure."

His father's voice was still low but it shook with anger. "I been hunting bear since before you was born. I ain't got killed yet."

The young man leaned back against a high rock and squinted through the finder on his camera. "Yeah, but you've gone off your rocker about Grizzlies, Pa. You ain't using good sense."

"You look out, telling me I ain't got good sense. I'll put you out of the house for good."

"No need. I'm going anyway."

"You'll go when I say so, not before. I need you on the place. Only reason I put up with you, I need a hand."

"I'm going, Pa. Maybe tomorrow. I made up my mind."

"Don't talk hogwash. Shut up now, or that bear'll hear us coming a mile away." He started into the narrow mouth of the canyon. "Come on, and try to keep still for once."

"I'm not going through that canyon."

The man's voice rose. "Then get out of here. I'm sick of you, Georgie."

"I'm sick of you, too, Pa." The young man straightened up. "I'll send you a postcard." He turned and went back down the trail.

His father watched him for a moment. Then he muttered something to himself and started through the canyon.

The silvertip didn't like having a man above him on the trail and another one below him. After a few minutes he climbed the hillside, and then cut off across a stretch of loose, sharp rock. He kept going for about 8 miles.

He heard no gunshots. Late in the day he found two coyotes feasting on the remains of an antelope that had died. The coyotes melted away into the shadows at his approach. He ate for some time.

Once, toward sunset, he thought he smelled man scent in the air, and he withdrew to the protection of a nearby butte. But after a while the scent was gone, and he returned to his meal, driving off the flapping ravens.

5

Almost three weeks went by before the silvertip ventured back to more familiar territory. There had been several heavy frosts, and below the timber line the hill-sides, dense with the dark green of fir and spruce and pine, were patterned now with the gold of western larches. On the lower levels an occasional mountain ash laden with red berries tempted the bear. Clouds of cedar waxwings rose up out of the mountain ash when the bear approached.

Winter was coming in early, and the bear was eating steadily in preparation for it. His coat was thick and smooth, and his weight had gone up to about 350 pounds. He was over 6 feet tall.

One day he went to look at the den he had used the winter before, but he saw recent bear tracks and smelled recent bear scent. Some bear, probably his sister, had already begun to prepare the den for winter. He would have to make a new one of his own.

He went back to the hillside where he had had his resting place early in the summer. Not far from there he found a partly cleared den that some other bear had once used or started to use. He went to work to clean it up.

There was a small, fast mountain stream not far away. Sometimes, when he went there for a drink, he lingered to watch a colony of beavers who were busy constructing a dam. At first one of the beavers slapped the water with his tail when the bear approached, warning the others of danger, and almost at once there was not a beaver in sight. But the bear was more interested in watching them than in harming them, and in time they ignored him and went about their business. Sometimes he would sit by the bank for an hour, watching them as they gnawed small trees and swam with the sticks and branches to their big cone-shaped house in the water. Some of them were busy storing food, bark from the willows that hung over the stream and

vegetation that grew along the bank. One day the bear sat so still that a red-backed mouse trotted right up to him before he realized his mistake. With a leap and a switch of his thin tail, the mouse climbed out of danger before the bear could catch him.

One evening on the way home, the silvertip met the pinto bear. The big bear dragged one of his hind legs when he

walked. The leg had been wounded by the hunter.

The pinto stopped short and growled when he saw the silvertip. The younger bear stopped too, and they eyed each other suspiciously. The pinto made a short lunge, as if he intended to attack, but the silvertip stood his ground, not wanting to fight the huge bear but not willing any longer to turn submissively aside.

The pinto lowered his head, snapping his jaws, waiting for the silvertip to turn away. Just beyond them, the trail was so narrow that there was room for only one bear; but where they were, it was wider and the land sloped upward into trees. The pinto expected the young bear to move off the trail into the trees. All bears moved aside for the pinto, even though he was now crippled.

He glared at the silvertip and clicked his teeth. He was almost three times as big as the younger bear. One lightning-fast jab of his paw could break the silver-tip's facial bones, or rake his throat wide open. But the silvertip's mother had been a dominant, aggressive bear, and he had learned to imitate her. He stood his ground.

The pinto was old, the oldest bear in that part of the forest, probably close to 45 years. Age had broken his teeth and blunted his claws, and the wounds inflicted by the hunter had crippled him and caused him constant pain. Perhaps for these reasons he chose not to challenge the young silvertip. He moved around him and went slowly, limping, up the trail. The silvertip stood perfectly still until the big bear was out of sight.

6

It was a cold, still October day, one of the last days that the bear would be eating before he began to fast for his winter sleep. All night a cold fog had wrapped the mountain, and now every branch and twig, every weed, was coated with heavy frost. The whole mountain seemed to be made of silver. Even the spider webs gleamed like metal threads, delicately wrought into a pattern.

As the silvertip went up the trail, the fog still hung on the mountain. In some places it had lifted 5 or 6 feet off the ground, in others it would part like a curtain for a few minutes and then close in again. The bear breathed in the cold, damp air, but there was no wind to bring him messages. He could hear no sound anywhere, except far below him the faint rush of the river.

He stepped silently and carefully along the narrow trail. There was a high, sloping bank at his left, with clumps of juniper growing out of the clefts between the rocks. On his right, fog hid the deep plunge hundreds of feet down to the river.

Suddenly he stopped. Ahead of him on the trail a figure was hunched. At first he didn't know what it was. Then a slight air current tattered the fog into streamers, and he saw that it was a man. It was the hunter, crouched close to the bank, his back to the silvertip. He had his gun aimed, and he was staring up the trail.

For a long minute the bear stood still. He could not see what the hunter was aiming at and his instinct was to retreat from this dangerous man with a gun; but it would be difficult to turn on the trail without being heard, and if he did and went down the trail, his back would be turned to the hunter. He stood where he was, waiting for the man to make some move.

After several minutes the man stirred slightly and raised the gun a little higher. The fog had shifted again, and now the bear saw what the man was aiming at. Some distance ahead of them, the old pinto bear stood on a flat rock that partly jutted out over the canyon below. He stood as still as a statue, staring out over the mountains. Fog drifted around him, so that he was sometimes partly obscured, sometimes entirely visible. He never moved. His head was lowered a little, and his hump and his big shoulders looked massive.

The fog swirled around him again, making him look like a great ghost. Then it cleared, and the silvertip heard the click as the hunter released the safety on his gun.

The silvertip roared. The big pinto swung around to face the trail. Startled by the noise behind him, the hunter fired and missed, and leaped up to face the silvertip. But the pinto was nearer to him. So the man turned and fired again at the old bear. This time he hit him in the chest. The first shot was followed by two more.

Roaring with pain the pinto charged down the trail, his crippled back leg making him lunge unevenly. The hunter tried to fire again but in his haste, his gun jammed. Terrified, he glanced back at the silvertip, who stood solidly in his way on the downward trail. There was nowhere to run.

As the badly wounded pinto hurtled toward him, the panic-stricken hunter dropped his gun and tried to climb the hill. He clutched desperately for handholds, but his fingers scrabbled at rock and loose dirt. At last he caught hold of a prickly juniper and swung himself partway off the trail. But at that moment the pinto reached him, and with a swipe of his paw he knocked the man back onto the trail. He began to bite the man's head and shoulders. The man screamed, and in a moment managed to get loose from the dying bear. He turned and ran a short way down the trail, then stopped, panting, a few feet short of the silvertip. The young bear made no move to charge him, just blocked his way.

The man's scalp was torn, and he was bleeding badly. He looked over his shoulder as the pinto gathered his strength and began another charge. With no sound except the sobbing of his breath, the man turned and leaped off the trail into the thick fog of the chasm. He instantly disappeared from sight, and there was no sound at all as he struck the rock-strewn river hundreds of feet below.

The old pinto stopped. He stared at the silvertip, his eyes almost blinded with pain and fury. He swayed and shook his head. Blood gushed from the gaping hole in his chest. A swirl of fog caught him, and for a moment the silvertip could hardly see him. Then the mist that had softened his outline cleared. The old bear shuddered violently and fell dead.

Later in the day, when the fog had lifted, the silvertip still stood near the old bear's body, driving off the scavenger birds who squawked and flapped just above his head. Toward evening it began to snow, a hard, blinding snow with big

flakes. In a short time, the pinto's body was covered with snow. And at last, just before nightfall, the silvertip left him and went back to the den. He would stay outside a few more days, fasting, adding the last touches of warmth and comfort to the inside of the den. Then he would go inside for his winter sleep. For the first time he would spend the winter alone. For the rest of his life, he would live as the old pinto had lived for so long, solitary and independent, in his mountains.

A NOTE ON THE GRIZZLY BEAR

The Grizzly, so called because of the grizzled or silvery guard hairs often found in his pelt, officially known by his Latin name of *ursus horribilis*, is second only to the Alaskan Brown bear in size. The full-grown male may weigh around 780 pounds, the female close to 500, though there is a record of a male who weighed 1,153 pounds. The maximum height for the male is about 85 inches, and for the female about 73 inches. The bears come in a variety of colors, from dark brown, and occasionally black, to a light blond. Not all Grizzlies have the silvery guard hairs.

The bear's range is normally 5 to 10 miles square, providing he can find food in that area. If necessary he will make a journey of as much as 70 miles in search of food. He likes high places, and often feeds along the timber line, especially in the fall. If he must, the bear can travel fast, up to 35 miles an hour for a limited time.

Although the bear is classed as a carnivore, he also eats vegetation. He hunts for small animals that are easy to catch, such as the marmot or the ground squirrel, and he often feeds on animals already dead. He is a good fisherman, and he is usually to be found wherever there is a salmon or trout run. He will also eat young birds and birds' eggs from nests on the ground, mice, frogs, and snakes. When he first comes out of his den in the spring, he eats bark, roots, berries, whatever he can find.

His winter sleep, which is not a true hibernation, begins when cold weather comes in the fall, usually in October or early November, and ends around May 30. Unlike the real hibernators, he may wake up from time to time during the long sleep, and he is easily disturbed.

The female does not breed until she is about 3 years old. The mating season is from approximately June 10 to July 10. She may breed once, or she may breed several times. The cubs are not born until January. Then there will be one or two of them, and they are born in the den. A newborn cub is generally 8 or 9 inches long and weighs about one-and-a-quarter or one-and-a-half pounds. By the time the mother leaves the den, a cub may weigh 12 or 15 pounds. A mother is very protective of her cubs, sometimes fighting off a male, who might kill and eat them. The mother stays with her cubs over one winter and until it is time for her to breed again; the cubs may stay together another winter, but beyond that time, they become solitary creatures, sometimes battling each other.

Grizzly bears are highly intelligent animals, and because of their size they have no natural enemy except man. Since their encounters with guns in the days of Lewis and Clark, the bears have learned to fear man. Except for the bears in and near the national parks in the western states, Grizzlies have almost disappeared everywhere but in Alaska and Canada, though a few still range the Rocky Mountains as far south as New Mexico. They are still legally hunted in Montana and Wyoming. If able to survive the hazards of man and disease and accident, a grizzly bear may live to be 40 or 50 years old.